Unsettled

Unsettled

REEM FARUQI

HARPER
An Imprint of HarperCollinsPublishers

Unsettled

Copyright © 2021 by Reem Faruqi

Interior illustrations © 2021 by Soumbal Qureshi

Library of Congress Cataloging-in-Publication Data

Names: Faruqi, Reem, author.

Title: Unsettled / Reem Faruqi.

Description: First edition. | New York, NY : HarperCollins Children's Books, [2021] | Audience: Ages 8–12. | Audience: Grades 4–6. | Summary: Young Nurah reluctantly moves with her family from Karachi, Pakistan, to Peachtree City, Georgia, but, after some ups and downs, begins to feel at home.

Identifiers: LCCN 2020044128 | ISBN 978-0-06-304470-8 (hardcover)

Subjects: CYAC: Novels in verse. | Immigration—Fiction. | Pakistani Americans—Fiction. | Family life—Fiction. | Muslims—United States—Fiction. | Swimming—Fiction.

Classification: LCC PZ7.5.F37 Uns 2021 | DDC [Fic]—dc23

LC record available at https://lccn.loc.gov/2020044128

Typography by Carla Weise
22 23 24 25 26 LSB 7 6 5 4 3
❖
First Edition

For Amma and Abba . . . and Nana, of course

In memory of Nana Abu, Pyarijan,
Dada, and Dulhan Chachi

Unsettled

PART ONE

Uprooting

Escape

I grab Asna's hand,
palm to palm,
nail to nail,
    and lean in,
but Nana's hand
yanks my shoulder.

Don't you know
about the father
who went in
to get the mother
who went in
to get the brother
who went in
to get the baby?

The sea swallowed them up.
These waves
*are **not** to be played in.*

But Nana ... I'm a swimmer!
Nana gives me a look,
a flash of gray-ringed eyes.
A look
that makes me swallow
my words up whole.

Best Friends

My grandmother Nana watches us,
so we stay on the sand.

After watching
camels roam in the surf,
their pom-poms taunting us,
a balloon seller bobbing by,
red yellow blue green circles
looking
d
o
w
n
at us,
an elderly beggar woman
(with too many wrinkles to count),
and black crows,
shrieking for food and company,
Asna and I trace our names
over and over,
watching the waves
slurp them up.

I watch Nana right back.

Beach Food

For lunch:
Soft mutton that my fingers shred easily.
Biryani rice.
Brown, saffron gold, white
ghee-soaked grains
that gently slip off my spoon.

For dessert:
A white box tied with string
Asna and I sneak our hands in.
Buttery biscuits from the bakery,
a dot of jelly in the middle.

For tea:
Roasted corn, its teeth
more black than yellow.
Chips saltier than the sea.

Teatime

When the sun is dipping,
and Nana goes in the villa to pray with Nana Abu,
we tiptoe in finally.

The waves pull hard
but we smile anyway
stuff our laughter in our cheeks
giddy with getting away with it.

After a few waves
guilt strikes.
We turn to tiptoe back,
but my glasses fall
and even though I try to grab them,
the sea sucks them up,
never to return.

The Perfect Day

If I could choose
a day
to live over and over,
I'd choose today.

Camel rides on the sand,
the feel of stiff fur.
Memories of the sun setting in our hair,
sandy eyelashes.

Home

After the bumpy ride home
from the beach
we are served
scoops of gold—
Nana's mango ice cream
and Baba's news.

The Worst Day

If I could choose
from all the days on this earth
to live over and over,
I'd skip today.

Tangle

Just when my grandmother Dadi's mind
becomes so tangled
that she doesn't remember
my name anymore,
Baba, my father, gets the news:
a job offer in America.

He says Yes
because my uncle is here to help.
He says Yes
because schools there are better.
He says Yes
because of "job security."
He says Yes.

The Yes slices our old world away.

We will travel.
Mile upon mile.
Mile upon mile.
While my grandmother's mind
tangles up more.
Tangle upon tangle.
Tangle upon tangle.

Math Class

While I wait
for my new glasses to be ready,
reading is fuzzier
but numbers are still sharp
in my mind.

The teacher taps her desk,
picks and flicks
chipped rosy polish,
the color of my gums,
while we are supposed to
be solving for x, a, and b.

But I am counting
hours,
     minutes,
          seconds.

How many seconds do I have
if I leave in 53 days?

Swift pencil marks
On paper
Calculate
53 days × 24 hours × 60 minutes × 60 seconds
= 4,579,200 seconds.

I like math
because there's always one answer.
6 + 7 will always = 13 (my age).
I like math
because numbers don't change their minds.
I wish Baba
wasn't like a number right now.
I wish Baba
would change his mind
and let us stay.

My Family's Outsides

Me

I have a bump
on my nose—
the doctor calls it
a deviated septum.

My nose is always stuffy,
and a little crooked,
and even though I don't want people
to notice my nose,
it is always making noise,
so it gets noticed anyway,
especially when it gets
extra stuffy
after I go for a swim,
which is my favorite thing,
ever,
which is every day.

My eyebrows are not
inverted delicate Vs like my father's
but straight bushy lines
like my mother's.

My face is practical,
too practical,
but it envies my hair,
a black mirror
that in the brightest sunlight
turns brown.

My hair is always smooth and silky,
it makes friends easily
with my fingers
and the comb.
If I choose to cover my hair,
like my mother,
what will my face envy?

My Big Brother

Owais, who is 2 years and 2 days
older than me,
732 days to be exact,
doesn't want to move either.
His eyebrows hug each other
as he pushes *dal* and rice
around his plate,
around and around.

Instead of packing,
he visits the swimming pool.
Diving deep

into the water,
over and over again.

Instead of packing,
he visits the tennis courts,
slicing the ball
easily over the net.

He slices the ball so hard
and so far
away,
that when the ball finally
hits the net,
he sinks to his knees
and doesn't have the energy
to get up.

Ammi: My Mother

Original owner of the thick bushy eyebrows.
My mother's brows are straight lines
like Owais and me.

If you were to pour tea,
and add a little milk,
and count 1, 2, 3, 4, 5,
that would be the color of
my skin.

If you were to pour tea,
and add milk,
you would need to pour,
pour,
pour,
and
count 1, 2, 3, 4, 5, 6, 7, 8, 9, 10
until the color of
my mother's skin.

My mother, Ammi, is prettier than me.
I know it in the way she lingers
at the mirror
and I don't.

Her delicate features
boast at more beauty
while mine
have already
accepted
who
they
are.

But there is one thing of mine
that is better than hers.
Her hair knots easily,
and mine never does.

Her smile doesn't
reach all the way
to her eyes
when she tries to sell us America.

Baba: My Father

My father's eyebrows are
the wings of birds
flying into the horizon.
Only when my father is mad,
they become like my mother's.
Now that we're moving,
from Pakistan to the United States of America,
they stay inverted.

Nana Abu

The father of my mother,
Nana Abu,
has two toes on his left foot
that hug each other
one a little in front
of the other
one a little behind
the other
that I call
hugging toes.
Even with his
hugging toes,

my grandfather does not really
give out hugs.
But when Nana told him
that we were moving,
his tree arms reached out,
long and loving limbs
gave me a side hug.

Asna

Is the tallest in the class,
taller than the boys,
taller than Mrs. Zakaria even.

I am the smallest in the class,
smaller than the teacher,
smaller than all the other boys and girls,
but when I am with Asna I am the loudest.
So Mrs. Zakaria tries to move my seat
f   a   r
from Asna.

Now that I'm moving,
my seat will be very very
f   a   r.

Now is Mrs. Zakaria happy?

Last Day of School

I make my eyes hard
scoot my chair
next to Asna
close the space
all the way
no inches left
not even a millimeter.
I look around
and dare Mrs. Zakaria
to say anything.

She doesn't.

Asna

Asna is my friend.
Not just any friend.
Not just a good friend,
but a best friend.
Asna,
who has a new baby sister,
says
but you have to
be here
but you have to
see her grow up . . .

Have
Have you
Have you ever
Have you ever said
Have you ever said goodbye
Have you ever said goodbye to
Have you ever said goodbye to a
Have you ever said goodbye to a best
Have you ever said goodbye to a best friend?

Visiting Grandmothers

Guilt slaps
the soles of my feet
when I run up the marble stairs
to the mother of my mother,
Nana's room.
Then I walk slowly
to Dadi's room.

Dadi

When I tell
the mother
of my father
goodbye,
she doesn't wish me
a safe trip
a happy life
lots of love.

Instead, she asks me my name.

Seeds of Hope

My grandmother Dadi may not know my name,
but every morning,
she scoops seed into her
palms that are
lined
lined
lined
and she scatters it
round the garden.
The birds are remembered.

When she's not looking,
I scoop a handful of seeds,
knot them tight in my *dupatta*.
I will pack these with me,
take them with me,
feed the birds there,
feed them
for her.

Nana

When I tell
the mother
of my mother
goodbye,
she hugs me so tight
holds me so long
my eyes feel hot.

She is lucky.
She gets to stay.
Her roots spread deep
and don't have to be uprooted
like me.

Did you know nasturtium flowers
don't like to be uprooted?
Their roots don't like new soil.

Nana

Should actually be called *Nani*—
mother of my mother.
But Owais's first word was Nana—
father of my mother.
So Nana
     Who is always giving us food
     Who is always giving us clothes
     Who is always giving us books
     Who gives us everything really
grabbed the word
and said
mine.

Nana

Superb
is what Nana says
about my art
when I join her
in the afternoons
underneath the veranda fan
to paint, draw, sketch.

When I have a brush
in my hand
or a pencil,
my insides breathe.

But now that we're moving,
Nana is too busy to paint, draw, sketch.
I can read her mind
through her quiet sighs,
slight wrinkles,
mouth stitched together,
so she doesn't say too much.

Still—
Nana's disapproval
is like charcoal on paper,
heavy and smudged.

They say children are more resilient than we think.
Nonsense.
Children are far less resilient than we think.

(Nana knows everything.)

My Grandmother
Nana's Hands

Pierced my ears
when I was a baby.

Fed me my first bites
of mushy *khichri*.

Now her hands stay busy
making clothes
for me before I leave.

Now her hands
buy yards of cotton cloth at the bazaar,
piping at the lace stall,
bring the cloth home,
soak the cloth in a plastic bucket,
so it doesn't shrink, of course,
dry it in the sun, and take it to the tailor,
then phone the tailor—
Are the clothes ready yet?

Then return to the tailor to pick up the clothes,
hand the tailor crisp notes,
rewash and starch the clothes,
before finally giving them to me,
perfectly folded and ready to be packed.

Fold your dreams and pack them too
while you're at it,
her eyes say.

With us gone,
what will her hands do now?

Blue Cocoon

Under the peach sky
under the crows cawing
under the veranda
by the garden
is the pool.

One thing
Owais and I do
no matter what
every day
is swim swim swim
in Nana and Nana Abu's pool.

Nana Abu floats like a tree
sways side to side.
Nana bobs up and down
down and up
in her swimsuit and *sari* petticoat
while Owais and I
swim laps
back and forth
forth and back.

Owais's arms and legs
have more rhythm than mine,
have more speed than mine,
he wins medal upon medal.

But still
we are the
Underwater Siblings.

Down at the bottom
of the pool floor
we are in a
a bright-blue world.
Safe
in our blue cocoon.
Can we stay here until
the clouds go to sleep?

They can't make us move—
can they?
But we must
move
the same way
we must
come up for air.

Motia and Mehndi

Before our l o n g flight,
Asna's fat *mehndi* cone
swirls green farewell paisleys
and her initials and mine
intertwined
on my empty palms.

I push my new glasses up my nose
to study my new hands.

Before our l o n g flight,
white fragrant *motia* flowers
are threaded together
in three delicate circles.
One circle of flowers
loops lazily over my ponytail.
Two circles of flowers
placed on my
too-skinny wrists
by Nana.

Polished petals
hinting
at New Possibilities.
At hope?

PART TWO

Replanting

On Land

Differences attack my senses.
The American airport has no smells.
The AC is strong.
The floor is carpeted.
The voices are bold.
The clothes are different.
And why is *everyone* wearing jeans?

settle

verb set·tle \se-təl\

Definition of SETTLE

: to end (something, such as an argument) by
reaching an agreement

: to make a final decision about (something)

: to move to a place and make it your home

My mother
laughs on the phone
and tells the mother of my mother
how well we are settling.

But Nana doesn't see
what I do.

Ammi's eyes still aren't smiling
when she laughs,
and her eye circles run deep.

Nana doesn't see
Ammi braiding her hair
with one hand
twirl bend loop
or
biting her nails
into crescents—
something she only does
when she's nervous.

Settled is
when your roots are strong
and spread out every which way
like that tree—oak?
in the hotel parking lot.
(I don't know
my American trees yet.)

Settled is
when it's hard to pull you up,
when it's easier just to leave you
exactly
how
you
are.

I am
dandelion fluff
ready to float
away.

If I could,
I would
float all the way back home.
I don't even need a breeze.

My roots are anything but settled.

Nurah Haqq

I used to be light
and free
before we moved.
My name means
"light" in Arabic and Urdu,
but I do not feel light or free
anymore.
I feel heavy,
even though
I will probably be the
lightest
in my class,
with maybe the
darkest skin color.
So much for light.

My Mother

Wears a *hijab*
neatly pinned
around her face.

Wears a hijab
because she is Muslim,
not because she is Pakistani.
Yet even when
she does wear jeans
and lightly lines her eyes with
L'Oréal instead of *kajal*,
I doubt they are lined
with American hope.

Before the move,
it felt like my mother was in color.
Bold.
Now she's in black and white.
Faded.
Her movements are smaller,
her smiles zipped.
Her "back home" accent is turned down,
like volume on a knob.
What more will she lose?

Language Barrier

But your English is so good . . .
is what we hear.

Yet

from the car,
when we order food
from McDonald's
fast
the way it's done in America
fast
they don't understand us.

So we learn
fast
to stop saying water
with a soft *t*—
instead with a hard *d.*

A hardness new to us.
But old to Americans.

We learn fast.

We learn
the supermarket is a grocery store.
A dustbin is a trash can.
A trolley is a shopping cart.

We learn to move quickly in line,
not linger.

We learn to not expect tea and snacks
everywhere we go.

Language

Pakistan is said like: Pack-is-stan
Muslim is said like: Muzz-lim.
Water is said like: Wah-der.
All wrong.

Pakistan is supposed to be "Pah-kiss-tahn."
In "Muslim," the *u* is supposed to be like *oo* in book,
the *s* a soft and gentle pout—
not a hard *z*
buzzing back at you.

Which Land Is Mine?

In Peachtree City, Georgia,
the trees touch the sky
and the air smells different.
The water tastes different too.
The wind is pure
and free
from exhaust.

Yet the sidewalks are empty.
The roads have only cars.

In Karachi, Pakistan,
the trees are shorter
like me.
The air has whiffs of exhaust
and mango juice is plentiful.
Rickshaws sputter on the roads.
A donkey here or there.
Scooters everywhere.
Sellers of every kind
selling
coconuts
birds in cages

balloons
towels.
They all
gather on the road.

Different melodies
all at once.
Even though their lives
are hard,
they seem free.

Yet America with
its pure air
and people stuck inside
all day
is known as
the land of the free.

Pakistan with
its free people everywhere
and dirty air
is known as
the land of the pure.

Hotel

We are in a hotel
and our bags are
sticking their tongues out
at us
half opened
spilling their contents out
just so.

Our room is ugly
with small windows
the color of spit
and Owais and I are
restless, trapped
even though it is sunny out.

Go get your Quran.
Let's read Surah Al-Kahf.
Ammi's voice is
too floaty,
too cheerful.

Owais's eyebrows hug.
His face is light enough to turn red.

Whoever reads Surah Al-Kahf
on Friday will have a light that shines
from one Friday to the next.

Go get it now,
commands Ammi.

You can't make me.

Her voice
is fragile poison.
What did you say?

I want to tell Owais
don't say anything.
Just sit down with me,
open your Quran,
and read Surah Al-Kahf,
the way we always did on Fridays.
The melodious words
of peace
rolling off
our
tongues.

Instead,
his voice is
dangerously quiet.
You can't make me.

Ammi raises
her palm
while I wait for the
stinging sound
of
skin to skin.
The hot slap.

You know,
here in America,
I can call the cops
and DFCS can take you away?

He walks to the door.
Tears pinch my nose tight.
I who never cry
in front of anyone,
never ever
find that my face
is wet.

Little

When we were little
and Ammi would tell us
to go pray,
we would listen.
But when we would put our foreheads
on the ground,
instead of praying,
we would look at each other
and whisper secrets.

Now,
I look at my brother,
and I don't know who he is,
or what his secrets are.

Stop

They both look at me,
surprised.
My tears
surprise me most.
I cover my face,
hoping the embarrassment
evaporates.
Relieved that their voices are
mute.

Owais, who was
on his way out,
stops
turns
changes his face.

Nurah, I didn't mean
to make you cry.
Sorry.
Ammi, I can't take it anymore.
I hate this place.
I'll read later.

And then he is
slamming the door
behind him,
gone.

My Family

Is beginning to fracture
one day at a time
while we are stuck
in this stuffy
hotel room.

Maybe when school starts
when the leaves
start changing
colors . . .
Baba has promised us
the leaves will change into
the colors of
hot spices:
cumin, red pepper, and turmeric.
Maybe then, things will get better.

Ammi Says

You should:
    Make your bed
    Go for a walk
    Pray on time
    Go find a pool

Go find a pool . . . ?
Owais and I
exchange a look.
If we find
a safe blue cocoon,
maybe then
our moods
will cool?

Where?

Where is a pool?
Where are the crows?
Where is the garden?
Where is home?

They're a 15-hour flight away.

PART THREE

Water

The Rec Center

A sigh of relief
even though it
smells of
stale socks
and warm sweat,
because most importantly
there is the smell of chlorine.
A pool.

Warm Welcome

I slowly
    d
       i
          p
the big
toe
of my
right foot
into the pool.
Bliss.

Blue Cocoon

Under the water
the bright-blue world
welcomes me
with a cool hug.
Under the water
Owais and I exchange
one watery smile.

If I just close my eyes
hard enough,
if I float just so,
I can almost imagine
I'm back
home.

Trophy Case

Between the locker rooms
is a shiny wall
with swimming medals and trophies,
and when we walk by the wall,
Owais takes a quick look.
But I take a
s l o w
look,
place my hands on the glass,
leave behind smudgy fingerprints,
but take my dreams with me . . .

TV

On the Olympics channel
Owais and I
tune in to swimming.
As I watch,
I hold my breath.
Exhale when
the race is over.
Owais flicks off the TV.

Keep practicing
maybe you can be in the Olympics . . . ,
says Baba
looking at Owais
the star athlete.

My mouth turns
the tiniest bit down,
so he adds
You too, Nurah!

I nod,
turn my lips back up again.
But the good energy in the room

that was swimming around us
is now drowning me.

What does it feel like
to be a winner?

School Morning

On my first day of school
when we climb into the big yellow bus
step by step
we don't know that Baba follows our bus to school
stop by stop.

Ammi tells us later
Baba wanted to make sure
we reached school safely.

I guess it's not just Ammi—
Baba worries too . . .

The First Day of School

The leaves *still* haven't changed colors.
I knew I was short at school,
but I didn't realize
how short I really was
until I saw Jason Flynn
the tallest boy in the school
and as I followed him
down the hallway
my head reached the bottom
of his book bag.

I knew I was brown,
but didn't realize
how brown I really was
until I saw so many
who were white and pink,
pink and white,
and only a handful of dark brown.

And although school just started,
and the bell rang only 7 minutes ago
(420 seconds to be exact),
I already feel like I don't belong.

Language Arts

Is a class
where I don't know where to sit.
So I stand by the classroom door
and double numbers
inside my head
to calm me.
1 + 1 = 2
2 + 2 = 4
4 + 4 = 8
8 + 8 = 16
16 + 16 = 32
32 + 32 = 64
64 + 64 = 128
I reach the number
1,024
when the teacher shows me
where to sit.

Language arts
is a lie.
There is no art
in here.
Just lots of punctuation

, . ! — . . . ; ?

And confusing questions
that can have
more than one answer.

Science Class

Relief.
Because we have
assigned seats.
Relief.
Because there is
a math problem
on the board.
Relief.
Because math problems
are safe
and have only
one
answer.

Hands

I am already solving
the math problem
in my head . . .
when *Hi, I'm Aidan,*
his arm reaches out.
Hi, I'm Brittany,
her hand shakes his.
This time he looks at me.
Hi, I'm Aidan,
his hand is out.
His hands waits.
I am so surprised
for a second
I don't know what to do.
I don't want to explain,
so instead my hand
reaches out slowly.
He smiles.
My fingers—always cold—
touch his.
His fingers
are warm
like his smile.

I forget to say my name.
It's Nurah.
But they don't ask.

I hope no more boys
try to shake my hand.
I'm Muslim,
I'm not supposed to touch boys
who aren't related to me.
Guys who aren't my brother,
father,
grandfather,
mother's or father's brother.
Aidan isn't any of those.

What would Nana say
if she saw me
shaking a boy's hand?

Math Class Decisions

The numbers draw me
into their world
inviting me with a wink
of + - ÷ and ×.
The numbers almost distract me from
seeing a girl
with a fat braid
who reminds me of Asna.

Coloring 101

In geography class,
there is a teacher,
brown-ponytailed,
with a too-big smile.

Welcome to geography.
Otherwise known as
Coloring 101.

Baba,
You lied.
I thought the schools
here in America
are supposed to be better?

Lunchtime

At lunchtime,
the girl with the fat braid
is sitting at a table
     loud with laughter,
     full of friends.
I realize
that I need her,
but she doesn't need me.

I button my lips,
keep walking past her table,
past *all* the tables,
and slink near the stairs.

Second Day of School

What did you say your name was again?
Aidan asks.
Nurah.
My name is Nurah.

I sneeze.
God bless you.
I don't know if
I'm supposed to say thank you,
so I say nothing.
To be safe.

Aidan

His skin is golden brown,
like smooth sand.
His eyes much lighter
than mine,
soft toffee brown,
and much kinder
when he offers me a
crooked smile.

Isn't he cute? whispers Brittany
when he gets up
to go to the restroom.

And when Brittany asks
that question,
Brittany Walker with her
blond hair and blue eyes,
I don't know why,
but I feel smaller than I am
and sad.

I don't feel like I,
Nurah Haqq,
with black hair and dark-brown eyes
am enough
    enough for Aidan?
And if I ever will be.

Lab Partner

For some reason
when it's time
to choose a lab partner,
Aidan smiles
his crooked smile
and chooses me,
not Brittany.
And I feel better than
I've felt
in quite a while.

Clothes

Nana has tailored
my clothes
for me.

Red piping.
3 buttons.
2 pockets even.
Floral print.

Colors bright
and happy.
Aqua blue
paired with
eggplant purple.
Ripe-mango yellow
paired with
unripe-mango green.
Rosy pink
paired with
bright orange.

Cloth so soft
it feels like tissue.

But then I hear the whispers
that scratch like nails.
Even though
I pair the *kurtas*
with stiff jeans, not *shalwars* . . .

Why does she wear clothes
like that
every day?
Why doesn't she wear anything
different?
I don't know how some people
go through middle school
dressed like that.

The colors of my clothes
are no longer happy.

In Walmart, the only
long-sleeve shirts
that are loose
that I like
are in the women's section.
No pockets.
No floral print.
No red piping.
Shirts rough like towels.

Dull like
the colors of
    crumpled litter on the beach.
Ugly faded brick.
Faded purple marker.
But I buy them anyway.

Autumn

The leaves have finally
changed into
a glory
of spices.
And our moods
have cooled
with the weather.

But even though Asna
emails and calls
and I
email and call,
she is far,
too far
away.

I am still
alone.
So alone,
even when we 4 are all
together
in 1 little hotel room.

Sweet in
Comfort Suites

Baba has booked us
an extended stay hotel
called Comfort Suites,
but I don't feel the comfort
(the sofa bed sags and groans)
and it's not sweet.

Baba plans for us to be here
for no more than
a couple of months
(60 days or less)
while we look for a house,
maybe a home?

Owais and I long
for a house
until we realize
every Tuesday
and Thursday afternoon,
the staff bakes and serves
melty circles of joy

in the lobby:
chocolate chip cookies.

The suites are becoming
sweeter.

Comfort in
Comfort Suites

We don't know anyone.
But now we know
Miss Polly and Miss Josefina
who wear stiff blue housekeeper uniforms.

In the corner of our suite
is a small black rectangle stovetop
where Ammi cooks food
where magic happens
where the taste of home
coats my tongue.

When Miss Polly or Miss Josefina say
Something sure does smell good
(it does!)
Ammi packs them curried rice
to take home.

Even though Ammi uses
frozen bags of vegetables
and fried onions from packets

and tomato sauce from cans,
we scoop the steamy golden rice
into our mouths
over and over
again.

The Ways of Rice

Ammi shows us
the ways of rice.
In Karachi we had a cook
named Zeeshan.
Now we must help Ammi.
We put 2 teacups
of rice in a pot
(the one with the
jiggly handle).
Wash with cold water.
Measure the water up
to 1 fingertip line
and cook on bubbly high.
Once the rice
swallows up the water
and it looks like finger holes
are poked in the rice,
Owais covers the pot
and sets the timer
for 10 minutes.
We wait wait wait
until
the *beeeeep!*

I fluff the rice
with a fork,
coat it with ghee . . .

Cooking coats us
with togetherness.

House Hunting

We see houses that are too big.
Some houses that are too small.
One house looks "just right,"
a room for me
a room for Owais.

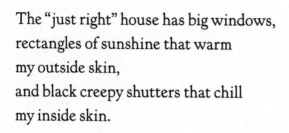

The "just right" house has big windows,
rectangles of sunshine that warm
my outside skin,
and black creepy shutters that chill
my inside skin.

My parents pray *istikhara,*
Oh God
I seek your counsel.
If you know buying this house
is good for me,
my religion
my life
then decree it for me.
If it's bad for me,
then turn it away from me
and give me something good
and make me satisfied with it . . .

My parents pray
they talk
they sleep on it
then they say Yes.

We get the "just right" house
creepy black shutters and all.

A New House

We are in the new "just right" house
finally
with carpets the color
of teeth.

We are scurrying
like roaches
unwanted visitors
because the plumber
is coming.

Quick
wipe the counters,
Quick
wash the dishes,
Quick
vacuum the crumbs.

But why?
We wonder.
Because we don't want the plumber
to think Muslims are dirty!

Ammi's hands pause from washing
and find their way
to her hips.

The air puffs my hair,
floats it,
as I sigh.

The plumber comes
and goes
and he does not take
off his shoes,
leaving red footprints
of Georgia clay
on the white carpet.

And we are the ones
worried
about
dirt?

Lunchtime

The loud chattering
of friends
who are not
my friends
scrapes at my soul.

I never know
where to sit
or who with.
So I sit underneath
the stairwell
in a triangle space
that is dark and small,
just like me.

In my last school,
I always knew
where to sit
and with who.
In my last school,
my name was known.
In my last school,
my voice was loud.

In this school,
I am mute.
In this school,
I am invisible.

Skype Calls

Late nights or early mornings
when Nana and Nana Abu call
when Asna calls
Boop Boop Boop!
Boop Boop Boop!
Happy sounds.
Even though the screen is small,
the house becomes a
home
full of laughter
and loud voices.
But when we say bye,
our house becomes
too quiet
too f   a   r
a house that is
7,995 miles away
to be exact.

Walking to
the Rec Center

On the walking path
golf carts speed by,
dogs pull people,
and bikers whiz by.
We hear
Hey y'all
How are you?
Hi
Owais and I
give each other a look
Who are these people?
Why are they saying hello?
People here must be really friendly
we think,
but then
Why don't I have
a friend at school?

Rec Center

The water is bright.
The water is blue.
It says
I am here for you.
Oh Water,
do you know
that you are my only friend?

The water scoops me into a hug,
laughter bubbles at me,
and floats me gently up high.

In the water, I'm the meaning
of my name—
Light.

Cold

Even though it's hot outside,
I hate
feeling the horrid cold
snaking into a ball
in the pit of my stomach
at school, especially at lunchtime.

But when the weather changes
one ordinary night,
I wake up
cold inside
and freezing outside,
and it's brutal.

I wear sweater upon sweater
5 total
just to feel warm
when I wait for the
bus.

Let's go buy you a proper winter jacket,
Baba says,
but still
it is not strong enough
to keep out the cold.

Karachi

Back home
the weather is
hot hot hot.
But in the evenings
when the sun gets sleepy
it gets cooler
balmy
and
breezy.
A tropical hug
before bed.

American Winter

Winter:
snips
cuts
the tips
of my fingers.
I am not made
for this weather.
I am not made
for this country.

Baba's Patience

We have a fireplace
that we are still learning—
a button to press
a switch to pull
to make a fire.

By the hungry orange licks,
Baba mends kites
and waits for
an invitation from the sky.

Birds

In Pakistan:
the birds are loud
morning
noon
night.

Here:
the birds are loud
only in the morning
only at sunset.

Here I am loud:
only in the morning
before school
only in the afternoon
after school.

After School

At the dining table
I find my voice.
With a few pencil strokes
I doodle America
away
by drawing the Karachi beach.
Angry wave
upon
angry wave.
We talk about
Nana and Nana Abu and Dadi and Asna
back home
and the world feels
smaller.
Happier.

I push away the
school day
flip my apple
upside down,
biting into
the red underbelly
creating a flower-shaped pattern.

Then pray *namaz*,
then homework,
then finally,
it's time to swim.

In the pool
we dive

      low.

We float high.
On the surface,
eyes closed,
I float my worries away.

Bright-Yellow Flyer

I see it
at the Rec Center
underneath the sunny window
winking at me.

I grab one
fold it into
one rectangle
two rectangles
three rectangles
four.
I place it at the top
of my swimming bag
with a smile.

Teatime

Why don't we both
try out for
the Center swim team?

Owais's face
is happy.

Owais is the
athlete,
the one
with the medals and trophies.
I am okay,
but not good enough
to win a medal
or a trophy
or anything really—
at least *not yet.*

But when I see
Owais's dark eyebrows
unstitched
I know I can win.
Maybe even a medal,

so that is why I ask.
That is why I say,
Let's do it!

*Maybe you can make
some friends,*
adds Baba.

Definitely!

Enthusiasm
is
contagious.

Skin

At swim team tryouts
there is skin
skin
skin.
Arms and underarms
legs and thighs.

I am wearing leggings,
a swim shirt with sleeves.
And even though I am covered
covered
covered
I am scrutinized.
The odd one out,
again.

Dollop of Hope

The next day
at tryouts
one girl is there
wearing tights
and long sleeves
too!

She stands by me.
Does she know
I need a friend?

Before we dive
leaving a trail of bubbles
like hope behind us . . .
I'm Stahr!
I'm Nurah!

Pep Talk

Coach Kelly's
hair is
    curly,
        bouncy,
            like the tentacles
                of an octopus.
But her voice is
low
and
rough.

If you make the team,
I expect
Winners
I expect
Medals
I expect
A strong team
I expect
You to do your best
I expect
Teamwork.
Any questions?

Stahr

Whose name has an extra *h*
but is pronounced like Star
finds me at school
before I go to
my safe triangle
underneath the stairwell.

Do you want to eat lunch with me?
8 words that change my life.

Stahr has freckles.
Not like me.
Stahr's teeth are covered in metal.
Not like me.
Her eyes are pale green and gray.
Not like me.
She wears long sleeves
at school
all the time.
Just like me.

But one day at lunch,
she pulls up her sleeves,

and shows me the yellow,
the purple,
and the blue.

My dad hits us with his belt,
and cusses at us.
Don't tell anyone, okay?

I am a good friend.
So I don't.

Camouflage

I always wished I
had freckles,
but seeing Stahr's,
I don't think I would want
that many.

If Stahr wears green,
her eyes are green.
If Stahr wears gray,
her eyes are gray.
It doesn't matter
what color I wear—
my eyes stay
dark dark brown.

Imagine

Underneath a sky
the color of promises
Stahr and I sit
at lunchtime
on a bench
in bright sunlight.
Imagine.

Difference

The difference between
having a friend
and not having a friend
can be told
from my face.

Before having a
friend
I would wear a mask
of silence.

I would not look here,
there,
everywhere,
but rather,
at the hallway floor.
Tile
after
tile.

With a friend,
I look here,
there,
everywhere.

With a friend,
my feet feel light,
like my name.

With a friend,
I don't have to stitch
my mouth tightly
together.

With a friend,
I let the corners
of my mouth
curl into a smile.

Swim Tryouts

Stahr swims like me
and
I swim like Stahr.
We share the same pace
arms slapping the water
feet kicking.
We talk about
how we want to make the team
how we want to win medals
and Stahr wants to know
How did Owais get so good?

We float lazily
and giggle giddily
until Coach Kelly claps
her hands
and barks
Okay, ladies,
less talking,
more swimming!

But this only makes us
laugh louder,
and Coach Kelly
offers us a little smile.

Strokes

It's all about the strokes,
says Coach Kelly.
You want your arms to
slice
the water
not slap.

This I can understand.

For art
with my pencil
I can press hard
to get darker colors
light strokes
for light colors.

For swimming:
quick strokes,
precise strokes,
to win.

Alyson

In geometry class,
Mr. Ferguson sings the
quadratic formula.
Negative b
Negative b
Plus or minus square root
Plus or minus square root
b *squared minus* 4ac
b *squared minus* 4ac
all over 2a
all over 2a.

While he sings
and I doodle,
the sunlight
is making friends with my hair.

My arms are so long they can easily reach
the tops of the cabinets to get a glass,
to drink wader not water,
but my legs are not so long,
I am the shortest,
always the shortest in the class.

And Alyson who looks like the person
on the cover of the magazine,
and whose arms and legs
and everything in between
are exactly the size they should be,
puts down her pencil and says,
Omigosh Nurah, your hair is so pretty.

Surprised, I put my pencil down,
and let my lips whisper, *Thank you.*

Owais

I have better hair,
but his face is better looking than mine.
If you take a loaf of oatmeal bread,
I am the brown heel of the bread.
He is the white inside.
His lashes are longer than mine
even though he is a boy.
His lips fuller
even though he is a boy.

When I was little,
I thought Owais and I looked alike.
But now when I hear the aunties talk about us,
my ears pay attention
and I realize
we don't look alike at all.

Aunties will smile wider
when he is around
will compliment his looks
the slice of his dimple
when they think he can't hear,

120

but they forget that
we can hear
much more
than they think.

Masjid

At the *masjid*
I am covered.
You can see just my face
and hands.
Here we are mirrors
of each other.
Everyone here is almost all brown—
different shades,
and I feel like I can breathe easier,
like I'm almost home.

With my forehead down
on the prayer mat,
cool and soft,
I pray for me
to make the swim team.
I pray for medals.
I pray for peace in Pakistan.
I pray for God to give me the world.
Ripe and glistening
a gift
in my palm.

At the masjid, no boys will try to shake my hand.
Here the girls will try to be my friend,
but I will see them looking over my shoulder.
Is Owais looking?
I talk about him just enough
to keep their attention.

Junaid

Owais's new masjid friend is named Junaid.
After basketball in the parking lot
when the boys are in a circle,
even though a circle has no point,
no leader,
he is the leader.
His laugh the loudest,
his eyes the brightest.

In my mind,
his name bounces
round and round.

Does Owais talk about me at all to him?
I wonder.

Hair

It is too long
and its weight
is bogging me
d
o
w
n.

At the salon,
I point to my chin,
like a girl in a magazine
confident and smooth,
to show the lady
how short I want it to be.

Sweetie,
is your mom here with you?

My head shakes angrily.
No.
Can I talk to her on the phone?
I am tired
of always being treated

like a baby,
but I mumble the number anyway,
a number that I don't even like
memorizing
because I miss my old number
back home.

I just wanted to make sure
it was okay to cut her hair so short.
She looks so young!

As she cuts and snips,
my anger evaporates.
But when the assistant
sweeps away my hair
smiles at the
silky black Cs
on the floor,
she says
I'm trying to grow my hair out.
Just like how your hair
used to be.

I don't smile back.

School

I get random
compliments
from random people.
But when Aidan
walks by me in the hallway
he looks looks looks
at me
just me
and says,
Nice hair, Nurah.
I now know the reason
for my haircut.

Stand Out

Coffee break! yells Coach Kelly
whenever she wants to give us
a pep talk.
Remember,
when you're in the water,
you want to STAND OUT.
Got it?
Stand out.
We nod
and shiver.

Yes,
we will
do our best
to stand out.

Fall Parent Conferences

Needs to participate more
is written under the comments.

She can't stop talking at home,
Ammi tells Ms. White.

I am tired of being told
I talk too much
or I talk too little.

Ms. White thinks
I talk too little.
Coach Kelly thinks
I talk too much.
Why can't they just let me
be?

Hi, Nurah!
This is my mom.
This is my dad.
Stahr says to everyone,
eyes gray today
because she's wearing gray.

Walking proudly
next to her parents.

I do not tell anyone
This is my mom
or *this is my dad.*
I try to walk a little in front,
sometimes a little behind.

Ammi is the only one
wearing a hijab
(seafoam green at that)
and even though I like the sea,
I really don't want
to call more attention
to us.

Why can't I just
blend,
like everyone else?
Why can't I just
blend,
like Stahr?

Amphibian

In water
I want to stand out.
But on land
I want to blend in.

On the Way Home

What a friendly child
your friend Stahr . . .
what nice parents too . . . ,
Baba and Ammi remark
and I hate
how anger
pools inside of
me.

To make them stop,
Her dad hits her, I say
and my mother's face is sad again.

Swim Team

My mother's face
My father's face
My brother's face
My face
are happy today
because we *both* made the team.
(Stahr too!)

In a red booth
we sprinkle pizza with red pepper.
In a red booth
my mother wears red lipstick.
In a red booth
the cheese melts long and liquid—
into joy.

PART FOUR

Planting Seeds

My Mother's Belly

The belly of my mother is
mostly flat
but inside it
there is a secret.

The secret
is the size
of a raspberry.

I am expecting a baby,
she says, her voice full of
hesitation,
but underneath the hesitation,
I hear hope.

I finally feel
light
like the meaning
of my name.

Back Home

Asna has a baby sister
whose hair smells like Cocoa Puffs
and when I held
the baby,
I knew
how to
curl my mouth
into
a sh-sh-sh-sh.
I knew
how to
bend my knees
up-down-up-down.
My body will remember
again.

Doubts

But later,
when I'm alone,
I wonder and wonder and wonder
and the wondering makes
me feel heavy and heavy and heavy
all over again.

Before Bed

Did we move to
America
just so you could have babies
who are American citizens?
Is that why we are here?
The question slips out
much louder than I meant it to
and I can taste the salty anger
on my tongue.

My mother looks up
while she braids
her hair with one hand—
twirl bend loop.
Her face tired,
so tired
that I feel sorry—
I wish I could iron
her wrinkles away.

My Father's Answer

No
No
No
No

That is not the reason
that we are here.
We are here because of
job security,
the schools are better,
more opportunities.
Don't you like it here?

Anger

When I was little
and I lost swimming races
against Owais,
I would cry tears
shaped like secrets,
salt mixed with chlorine
behind my goggles.

I would throw my towel
call him names
churning the sadness
into anger.
Because isn't it easier
to be angry
than sad?

Swimming

The next day,
sunlight
brings
me
hope.

At times, I don't
understand the moods
of my heart.

But today
is easy.
Owais and I dive
high from the board
deep into the pool.

Everyone swims
(Baba too!),
except our mother,
whose face is
yellowy and who
doesn't like the smell of chicken
or spices

(or anything really)
so we pick up fish fillets
(the only thing that could be *halal*
on the menu)
through McDonald's
drive-through
on
the
way
home.

The Moment

The moment the ultrasound technician
tells my mother,
I am eating an *aloo kabab* sandwich at school,
Owais is solving for x,
and our father has just made a big sale.

Teatime

I spread the butter
just so,
bury it under jam,
am slicing the crusts off my toast
when my mother says
I'm not having a baby anymore.
I stop slicing.
On the ultrasound, they saw an egg sac,
but there was no baby inside.
Ammi, I don't understand.
This means there is a baby's home,
but no baby.

I understand the baby.
It didn't feel like the egg sac was
home.
It, too, didn't want to join us
in a place that doesn't feel like
home.

PART FIVE

Sprouting

The House

That doesn't feel like home
yet
is changing.
The sink once hungry
and hollow
is now swollen,
throwing up dishes.
Dust hugs the corners.
Stubborn crumbs
stick to feet.
I squirt soap
into the shape of a
heart
onto a sponge.

How can I
take care of a baby
when I can't
even
take care of a house?

Ammi's voice is
a cracking eggshell.
Before her face gets
runny,
she walks away.

Fact: I have never seen
my mother cry.

Raspberry

I never liked
the taste of raspberry
anyway.

Google

A blighted ovum
known as "anembryonic pregnancy"
happens when an egg
(a fertilized one)
attaches itself to the wall of the uterus,
but the embryo doesn't develop.
Cells develop to make the pregnancy sac,
but they don't bother to make the embryo.

Baby Sizes

Mustard seed.
Peppercorn.
Orange lentil.
Raspberry.
Peeled almond.
Cherry.
Green olive.
Fig.
Lime.
Banana.
Squash.
Mango.
Corn.
Coconut.
Pineapple.
Watermelon.

Nurah Haqq

I am a little sister
who was never meant
to be
a BIG
sister.

Skype

When Nana and Nana Abu call,
I tell them the news
news that was once good
now bad.

Nana's lips get small,
face turns down.

Verily to God we belong
and verily to God we return,
Nana Abu says.
Even though it's all he says,
his voice,
his words
are pieces
breaking
into the sky
swooping
d
    o
       w
           n
hugging Ammi and me.

Fajr Prayer Before Sunrise

I know it's bad
because Ammi
doesn't bother to wake us up early
at the white thread of dawn
to pray.
And I,
the lover of sleep,
sleep sleep sleep,
wake up with tension
nibbling my stomach.

Nana's Worries

When Nana calls
and asks how my mother is,
I tell her fine *alhamdulillah*.
I don't tell her
how she really is.
I think the way Nana
shrinks her mouth,
raises her eyebrows,
sighs,
she knows too.

Swim Meets

My skin
tingles all over
feet flex
arms swing

Coach Kelly
barks
Swim your fastest.
When you do freestyle,
and you're not breathing for air,
keep your head still.

Make sure your eyes are
at the bottom of the pool—
focused.
Don't look around
comparing yourself
to others—
especially when you're in
the middle of a race.
That'll make you lose your focus!

Got it?
Before thinking,
I pump my fists
and yell
YES!
Stahr giggles.

Coach Kelly's mouth
smiles wide.
I like your energy, Nurah!

Where Is My Mother?

Before, Ammi would
come to our swim meets
and watch me
always finishing right in the middle.

Before, Ammi would
come to our swim meets
and watch Owais swim
always finishing first.

Now, Ammi doesn't come.
She says her head hurts.
Does her stomach hurt too?
Does it miss the baby?

Almost Neighbors

Stahr lives only 8 houses away from me
but she doesn't know how long she's going to live
     there.
My mom is looking for a place away from my dad...

Stahr eats dinner at 5
and we eat dinner at 8
and tea at 5.

So when her mom is late
from work,
Stahr comes over
and waits to eat my mother's *samosas*,
which are perfect hot triangles—
golden-brown pastries full
of spices, meat, and oil.

But lately,
my father is still
at work
making money
working hard to keep
"job security,"
and my mother stays in her room.

Stahr asks
When are we going to have samosas?
Where's your mom?

I let the words slip out
heavy
My mother
had a miscarriage.

And Stahr who has too many freckles
and too many words
stays silent.

The Next Day

Stahr's mom
rings the bell
at 5:33 p.m.,
and we still don't have samosas,
or tea,
or anything really,
and *sorry* hovers
at the edge of my tongue.

But before I can say anything,
Here's a casserole, she says.
I've never had a casserole before,
and when I peek at it
underneath the foil
the yellow layers
muddle me even more.

She asks to see my mother
Ammi, someone is here to see you . . .
And Stahr, who is just Stahr,
not a big sister,
or a small sister,
or any sister,

whispers,
Four.
My mom had
four miscarriages
before she had me.

Teatime

When Stahr's mother
is over,
samosas are fried quickly,
jaldi se
tea brewed,
and my mother is not in her room
anymore.

Plans of Penelope

Monday Wednesday Friday
are the days that Stahr's mother visits.
Penelope,
whose hair is orange,
but here they call it red.
And instead of samosas
they nibble on Munchkins
that she brings
and I see my mother
becoming who she once was.

Staying Together

Fajr
the prayer of dawn
Zuhr
the prayer of noon
Asr
the prayer of afternoon
Maghrib
the prayer of sunset
Isha
the prayer of night

Once more,
my mother starts to wake us up
for Fajr
and I don't feel
the tension nibbling
anymore.

The other prayers
we pray together
and stay together
too.

The Surprise

Baba,
whose hours
are not so long anymore,
now that we are having teatime again,
now that my mother is *almost* herself again,
tells me he has a surprise for me.
Two big brushes.
two cans of paint,
the grayest blue,
to match the ocean waves,
he says,
and a rusty gold orange,
to match the sand.

Baba knows
I miss the beach in Karachi,
and am tired of the walls
white white white,
so we begin,
and now whenever I enter my room,
I hear the waves,
and smell the sand.

Baba hangs up hooks
with a hammer
and a bearded smile.
For your clothes
and medals
one day!

Leftover Paint

Our "just right" house
no longer has creepy black shutters,
but shutters that match the ocean.

Art Class

When I doodle,
my mind forgets
all that is happening
around me,
the bad
and the good
and the in-between.

My doodles
become sketches.
And when I write
in my journal,
the words and pictures
play and flirt
with each other.

I linger
over the paper
the way my mother
lingers over the mirror.

My Art Teacher

Ms. White
gives us a project
to draw a self-portrait.
I am forced to look
in the mirror
and draw, draw, draw.
Shadows of the eye,
bushiness of the brow,
hollows of the bone.
B+ is the grade I get.

Our next project:
Make a collage of a special place
that has meaning to you.
So I glue, cut, draw
crushed pink tile
hungry green plants
bold blue pool
by Nana and Nana Abu's garden
and get an A.

I wonder
what was wrong
with the picture
of me?

For the final project
draw yourself
for a self-portrait
but with something unexpected.

The class grumbles.
She pushes up her glasses
holds up a finger.
Draw what feels good.
Surprise me . . .

The Words of
Ms. White

I won't remember
your name
long after you're gone,
but if you have a piece
of art that's memorable,
I will always remember your work.
Always.

I want to be remembered.

Swim Meets

Owais and I
are used to Ammi
not coming anymore
but last time
Baba came,
and Ammi too.
Ammi's face was tight
Baba's face was loose
but when Owais won,
her face became
loose and lovely
and I wished that
I was a winner too.

Swim Meet

If I watch the ways of winners,
watch them hard enough,
maybe I will learn.
Once Owais swims lazily
in second place.
Way behind.

I am growing bored watching.
But suddenly near the end,
his pace
picks up . . .
I gasp as
his arms
slice the water
feet a blur
and suddenly
he is in first place.
I am hooked.

How did you do that?
My features incredulous
It was easy.
He shakes off the water

with a smile.
Now that he is back in the water,
his dimpled smiles come easy.
Too easy.

It's not fair.
Does he know how badly
I want to win?

Extra Sleep

Is like scraps of frosting
to me.
Irresistible.
But now on weekends
at the white thread of dawn,
I no longer sleep in.

Instead I head to the pool—
Stahr sometimes joins me.
We dive in
and practice.
Easy for Owais,
but not for me.
I do it anyway.

You need to work on your
technique,
says Coach Kelly.

I learn to slice through the water
not slap it.

I learn to make my feet
flutter into a kick.

I learn to breathe
every 3 strokes.

I learn to e x t e n d my arms,
catch the water at the top of my stroke,
rotate as I breathe.

I learn the perfect flip turn
to streamline off the wall.

I learn to reach forward
into the blue.

Afternoons

On a day
when the sun peeks out,
after Stahr and I swim,
we head to Baskin-Robbins
for scoops
of ice cream.

Stahr gets pistachio
one day,
strawberry
another day,
chocolate
another day,
and I get cookies and cream
all the days.

At Baskin-Robbins
Aidan works
behind the counter
sometimes.

Hi, Nurah!
he says with a crooked smile.

Who *is that?*
Stahr asks.

I whisper to Stahr about how
Aidan chooses me
in science class.
Stahr tries
to whisper
how she chooses
Mason in math class.

Even though I have never
heard his name
I know he must be important
because Stahr actually whispers
when she says his name.
When I am with Stahr,
secrets spill out
in seconds,
secrets I didn't even know
that I had.

By the time I have
talked
talked
talked
to Stahr,

My cookies are all melty.
No longer hard
mixed with soft.
Maybe that's what moving is like:
all the hard bits
eventually go away.

Help

Ammi's eyes are no longer foggy
but clear and focused.
So when Penelope comes over for tea
freshly bruised and watery-eyed,
Ammi serves steaming chai and questions.
What are you going to do?

Too long a silence.

A heaving sob.

I've been saving for a place.

Ammi puts two hands around Penelope's hands,
whispers
I'm going to help.

Delayed Teatime

While Stahr's dad works,
Ammi helps Penelope.
I help Stahr
fold and pack their clothes
and dreams away . . .
         for later.

Getting Better

Sometimes my dives
are crooked.
I close my eyes
wince
before diving in.
A broken dive.

When I race,
sometimes the water
is not my friend,
even though I try so hard.

You're bringing your arms
out of the water
too soon.
Follow through with your strokes.
Trust the water,
says Owais.

So I do.
Slowly,
slowly,
I am getting better.

I know this because
Owais high-fives me
Stahr hugs me
and Coach Kelly
smiles wider when I finish
my laps quicker
beating the clock
second by second.

Coach Kelly tells me
if I keep it up,
I will start winning soon.

I am the water,
buoyant with hope.

PART SIX

Rot

Bullied

Now that Ammi
is herself again,
she is back to what she does best:
worrying.

Ammi worries about us,
too much.
She buys us brand-new swimsuits
that smell like Walmart.
She packs us school lunches,
rolled-up *parathas*,
fried aloo kababs,
thermoses of rice
that tease us of home.

Are you being bullied?
No, we say,
because we aren't.
We smile big,
too-big American smiles,
to reassure her.

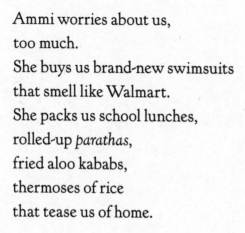

But
if she were to ask me
about the man
the man on the bus,
I would have to
say Yes.

The Bus

The bus is a friendly yellow.
On the bus is a man.
The man on the bus is a monitor.
He is almost whole.
He has 2 legs.
2 eyes.
2 feet.
2 ears.
2 nostrils.
1 arm.
1 hand.

Jay

On the bus is Jay.
Jay like the alphabet,
Sandwiched between *I* and K.
A, B, C, D, E, F, G, H, I, J, K . . .
Jay has eyes the color
of a swimming pool.
A dangerous one
I wouldn't want to jump into.

Jay and Cal are a team.
They whisper
to the man on the bus.

Did You Know?

A wedding ring
is worn
on the left hand?

The Incident

Jay and Cal do not whisper
anymore.
Their voices are loud.
Do you wear a wedding ring?
Can you shake hands with your left hand?

Their faces
change.
Their lips
smirk.
Their voices
laugh.

They laugh
All
The
Way
Home.

Mr. Tim,
the bus monitor,
stutters,

face turning red,
and looks out the window.
All
The
Way
Home.

I Wish

My skin stings
hot with anger,
but is too brown
to turn red.

I wish I could say something,
do something,
stop them,
but how?

I just look outside
at the trees.
Silent witnesses.
Just
Like
Me.

Sunday School

Whoever sees evil,
change it with his hand,
and if he is not able to do so,
then change it with his tongue,
and if he is not able to do so,
then with his heart—
and that's the weakest of faith.

I am the weakest.

Pep Talk

Coffee break! yells
Coach Kelly,
her arms
waving us over
even though
there is no coffee
just puddles
of chlorine water.

By the pool
we huddle
shivery and warm,
warm and shivery.

Don't forget
be like an octopus!
An octopus is not only quick
in the water.
An octopus is highly
intelligent.
An octopus knows
how to free itself
from difficult situations.

An octopus knows
how to soar
through the water.

I want to be
like an octopus.

Courage

Ms. White
arranges dying flowers in vases
walks around the room
in shoes that make no noise.

Ms. White gives advice as she peeks:
 Soften your edges . . .
 Notice the angles . . .
 You could add more here . . .

Behind me she stops
quiet
pushes her glasses up.

Her mouth lies down in thought.

I think she is surprised by
how I hold my charcoal
 easily
how I press down
 dark
how shapes and shadows appear
 clear

200

It takes courage to be so
bold.
Nice work.

Time

I hate riding
bus 11-269.
I hate stopping by
Blueberry Hill.
The stop adds 10 minutes
to our ride home.
10 minutes.
600 seconds.
Enough time
for anything
to happen.

Temper

In first grade,
Ms. Chowdhury made me sit next to
Ahmed Anwar.
A good girl
next to a bad boy.
Why don't teachers
change their tactics?

He threw my favorite
Little Mermaid
pencil case
down to the ground.
I gave him a look.
The second time
I told him to stop.
The third time,
I pounded
the back of his head,
right next to
the gentle circle
of his cowlick,
Pound, pound, pound,

down to the ground,
until I got dragged out
to the hallway
by Ms. Chowdhury.
Good Girl no more.

Inside

When I get mad,
I am not like
the water in a rice pot
simmering slow.
I am calm
calm
calm
and then I explode.
I am a teakettle
waiting to scream.

The Incident

Tension takes bites
out of my stomach.
At first nibbles,
but then bites.

Jay and Cal
are bending their arms
into stumps
waggling them
back and forth
laughing quiet and loud
all at once.

Even though my face is calm
like a lake,
with no ripples at all,
my face becomes a wave.
Tidal.
Wild and furious
all at once.

SHUT UP!
SHUT UP!
ACT YOUR AGE.

My voice is so loud,
such a surprise—
it
shuts
them
up.

Tomorrow

I fidget at the bus stop.
I am so scared
of what they will do today,
of what they will say today.

Owais is so lucky he is 15,
and that his friend Michael Lee is 16
and drives him to high school.
I feel so alone.
But before leaving, Owais
nods at me.
Is he trying to say
Everything will be okay?

Aftermath

Today
Cal and Jay
don't even look at me.
Not a peek.
They don't look at
Mr. Tim either.
The edges,
corners,
of my heart
feel lighter.

TERRORIST ATTACK

We can't focus
on our homework
because the words
stare angrily
in WHITE CAPITAL LETTERS
from the bottom
of the TV screen.
I don't like
the way
they are saying
Muslim
on TV.

Owais throws down
his pencil.
It's ironic, isn't it?
Islam means peace.
I guess the shooter
didn't really click
with that part.

The faces of my parents
look old and tired
and their sighs are
those of old people.

My father's face is still a frown
and his eyebrows
inverted Vs no more.
Please pray for the victims.
Be careful when you are
out and about.
You never know
when someone will look at you
and because they may think
you believe
what that idiot does,
they may
snap.

Knock on the Door

The next day,
when we are in school
and my father is
buttoning the third button
on his shirt,
there is a knock at the door.

The man's shoulders
are as wide as a refrigerator,
his waist a narrow bucket.
Sir, can you step outside?
My father asks why.
Again
Sir, can you step outside?
Then
I'm from the FBI
I need to ask you some questions.

Although my father's
eyebrows change
from delicate inverted Vs
into straight lines,
he asks

212

Why don't you come in?
The man whose shoulders
are as wide as a fridge—
his eyebrows become inverted Vs,
Sir, are you sure?
If I step inside,
and I see anything,
anything,
I can arrest you.

My father's answer
is easy:
I have nothing to hide.

My mother's voice
is gentle:
Would you like some tea?

Don't they know yet?
You don't have to be nice
to everyone in this country.

Facts

In Peachtree City,
it is sometimes colder in February
than in December.
It rains often.
Thunder.
Lightning.
Sometimes when it rains
hard enough in Peachtree City,
the electricity goes.
Just like in Pakistan.
In the darkness,
I am reminded of
home.

But today, it is rainy
and cold
so I cannot eat outside
with Stahr,
but Stahr is not here
because she is
getting the metal
on her teeth
tightened.

Inside the cafeteria,
a blur of faces,
I don't know
where to sit.
My insides feel
tight.

No one else
except Stahr
has said those 8 words to me
Do you want to eat lunch with me?

I square-root numbers inside my head
100 . . . 10
81 . . . 9
64 . . . 8
49 . . . 7
36 . . .
to calm myself.
I am only at 36 when . . .

A whispery voice.
Where are your friends today?
Cal is in front of me.
Probably no one
wants to sit with you
or your people
anymore.
His face is a chewed-up sandwich.

My insides become ice
my cheeks become fire
I am too brown
to become red.

I open my mouth.
But this time—
the words are stuck
inside me.

Y'all need to find a seat . . .
Ms. White is on lunch duty
walking with purpose.
Cal smirks,
Good luck with that . . .

Ms. White turns.
I scuttle out of the cafeteria,
plan to go back to the triangle space
underneath the stairwell
to eat my lunch
alone
again.

A tap on my shoulder
I look up

Up
Up
at a tall girl
I saw what happened.
She pushes her braids
behind her ears
a warm smile
brown sugar skin.
I'm Destiny.
You can eat with us . . .

I follow her.
Knots loosen
from my tongue.
Thanks . . .

Inside the cafeteria
the lights are too bright
But Destiny
walks right by Cal
too close.

You'd better leave her alone . . .
She is much taller
than Cal,
much wider too,
she holds her breath in,

looks down at Cal,
with scowling eyes.

Cal's face becomes
sour,
pinched.
He looks at me
hard
then walks a   w   a   y.

Art Class

Blocks of paper
creamy white,
charcoals smoky,
fat pastels,
welcome me on
Tuesdays and Thursdays.

In math there's only one correct answer
which I like
but in art there is no wrong answer
which I love.

A line can be swirly or straight.
A circle can be perfectly round
or turned into an oval.

Math I can do quickly
But art
I do
s l o w l y
on purpose.

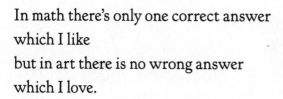

After the Terrorist Attack

The FBI officer
makes sure
to knock on all the doors
of the neighbors
before leaving
to ask questions
about any suspicions
they may have.

Does my father's skin,
beige like the grass
that has died in winter,
make you suspicious?

The voice of my mother
tired of being gentle
is now tight—
Assalamualaikum, Nurah,
Wa-alaikum-as-salaam, Ammi,
How was your day?
Fine.
Hidden words fill the air.
I don't tell her about Cal

picking on me
in the cafeteria.
I don't want to worry her.
I have a feeling she worries enough
by the way she peeks in the mirror
and loosens her hijab
ever so slightly,
before she leaves
the house.

PART SEVEN

Budding

Looks

It is important to note
that my skin is
dark
like the heel of oatmeal bread
while Owais's skin is
light
like the center of oatmeal bread.
We do not look alike
are not recognized
as brother and sister.

Jealousy

Coach Kelly praises Owais
                    all
the
time.
Owais is always
first.
I am almost always
in the middle.
When Owais wins,
Coach Kelly smiles big.
When I finish in the middle,
Coach Kelly smiles small.

Today, in our race,
I forgot my technique.
50 yards of me
slicing through the water,
my rhythm is off,
my arms and legs thrash
and
I am last.
Behind my goggles,

I can feel the familiar
pricking
of tears.
Why can't I be more like him?
When will I win?

Owais's Room

By his mirror
smirks
a
shelf
that
shines.

By his mirror
smirks
a shelf
full of
trophies
and
medals.

By his mirror
I am invisible.

By his mirror
if my insides
were visible
you would see

anger
bubbling
underneath
my skin.

Extra Practice

That is all you need,
reassures Owais,
my Underwater Sibling.

But I am already practicing extra
in the mornings.

Come with me
on the weekend
I'll show you some pointers,
Owais's slice of dimple smiles.
He tosses another medal
too easily
onto his shelf.

I shouldn't have said Yes
while my anger bubbled.

Star Athlete

Coach Kelly smiles
a big smile
to see us at the pool
on the weekend.

He's my star athlete!
she boasts to
the other coach there.

Owais is tall
has swimmer shoulders
and a swimmer waist
I am small and
don't have much
of anything.

Coach Kelly doesn't
see me
or maybe she does
but today
she doesn't really
see me.

Instead of Pointers

From the very top of the diving board
Owais is diving
high to low
high to low again
a flip here
a flip there
and there is a girl
with pink-painted lips
who looks up
smiles and claps.
If I were to do
the same dive,
she would not clap
for me.

Owais is
a better diver
a better swimmer
better in looks
and most things
and sometimes when
I'm with him
I fade
away.

232

If I were to sink
to the bottom
of the pool,
nobody would notice.
They would be too busy
looking at Owais
diving and
diving again.

The girl with pink-
painted lips
waves to Owais
before he goes
to the locker rooms.
He waves back
and I roll my eyes.

False Promises

Owais
didn't show me
any pointers.
Owais
didn't teach me
anything.
Owais
didn't do
what he was supposed
to do.

Before the
Locker Rooms

Out of the corner
of my eye
I see two of them
with football-player bodies.
They exchange a look
before they frown at Owais,
who still has a smile
on his lips.

They walk toward the girl
with the pink-painted lips.
That jerk needs to stop showing off.
I see one nudge the other.
I know, right?
smirks the girl
with the pink-painted lips.
She's looking
straight at me.

Do you know him?
she asks.

I don't really know him.
Not anymore.
I let out a laugh
that doesn't sound
like a laugh.
I let out a shrug
that doesn't look
like a shrug.

I let my mouth become an O
let my answer s l i p
out easily
too
easily.
Nope.

Locker Rooms

I should call Owais back
before he goes
inside the locker room
but he isn't paying attention
to me.
So
I
let
him
go.

Girls' Locker Room

Underneath the shower
drip drop drip
runs shower water

Drip drop drip
run my tears
not from
the chemicals
of the pool,
but from
the chemicals
of my heart.

And although
the water is hot,
my tears
run cold.

I try to wash
the worries away
scrub my fears
lather the pesky voice
that says

What kind
of person,
what kind
of sister
are you?

Waiting

I am waiting
for too long
outside the locker rooms
on the too-hard bench
and the two guys
who are tall tall tall
and wide wide wide
come out
laughing.

The girl
with the pink-painted lips
smirks at them
All done? she says.

I am stuck
waiting
waiting
waiting
for Owais.

Where is he?

Guilt nibbles at my stomach.
I stood up
for the bus monitor man,
but for my brother who
has 2 arms
and is better than me
at everything
I didn't call back.

When trouble
was thick in the air,
heavy in my ears,
I just watched
and waited.

Invisible.

Probably

He is probably just taking
a long
long
long
long
long
shower.
Right?

Lifeguard

Turning out the lights
my tongue is swollen
with tension.
My words are dry.
My brother hasn't
come out yet,
can you check on him—
please?

Stretcher

Under a sky
the color of
broken promises
the body of
my brother
is lifted out
of the locker room
in a stretcher.
His face
is puffy
and discolored.
I feel so
so
so
alone.
Why did
I let him go?

Hospital

At the hospital
my parents will
demand
Who has done this?
Why did they do it?
But I will
just shrug.
The words
clogged in my throat.

Sorry

He cannot hear me.
At least I think he can't . . .
I hold his hand,
I'm sorry
I didn't warn you.
More sorry
than you can
imagine.
The sorry
loosens my tongue.
The sorry
teaches me that next time—
if there's a next time—
I will know what to do.
I will know what to say.
I will
I will always
I will always say
I will always say something.

Fighter

When my brother wakes up,
his face is still a little colorful.
Owais, what happened?

*Nurah, I told them
I'm not a fighter,
but they wouldn't listen.
They wouldn't listen . . .*

Doesn't he know
the day we came here
we were made into
fighters?

Home Visit

Coach Kelly
comes to our house
and words like
> *surveillance cameras*
> *file a report*
> *justice must be served*

are written by Baba
on bright-yellow paper
served on the table
right next to chai
next to Owais's
emergency room
discharge papers.

Words fill up
the paper.

For My Brother

Before I felt
bubbles of anger.
Now I feel a
Water f
        a
        l
        l
        of regret.

For my brother,
I churn my apology into action.

I bring him steaming bowls of dal,
fresh stories of back home,
a pile of laundry
with socks matched
toe to toe.

I tell him he doesn't look so bad,
wait for him to smile,
but he's not ready yet.

Later

His face will become
the right color.
He will be fine.
Handsome again.
The two boys
will be reported
but they will come back
to the Rec Center
unfazed
and my brother
my brave
diving brother
will stay away from
the blue cocoon
of water.

PART EIGHT

Wilting

In America

I will look
for my grandparents
by habit
even though I know
they are back home
in Pakistan.
I realize
when I am in
the checkout line
helping
my mother
(always helping)
bananas
eggs
cans of tomato sauce
(for curry)
that I don't see
old people
here.
Where do they hide?

Here I see
young
and middle aged.

Only later when I join
Key Club
and have community service
I finally see
the old people
in nursing homes
rocking on chairs
staring into space
not being served
crispy samosas
not having their feet
massaged
not being visited.
Just staring.

Dadi

When Baba
says that Dadi is going to visit
to see a few doctors,
my heart lifts
to the top
of my short hair
I will see her soon.
But it drops again
to the bottoms
of my feet
when I remember that she
won't remember
my name.

Airport

At the Atlanta
international terminal
anticipation bubbles
around me.
There are people
who have light skin
the color of milk
with a drop of tea,
medium skin
the color of milky tea,
and dark skin
the color of tea
without a drop of milk.

People who are all
looking around
hungry for family.

I am holding my sign
Welcome Dadi!
On purpose
I left out
Home

because America
is not a home
for Dadi.

When Zaidu Chacha
and the attendant
walks Dadi out,
we wave big.
But Dadi
sees us
has to be guided over
to us
and when she sees us
her arms pat
the bones in my back,
and I smile big
because she must
remember me,
but then she
asks my name.

Babysitting

One Friday a month,
my neighbor Ms. Grayson asks me to babysit
her kids.

For dinner,
I feed them
    sticks of fish
    trees of broccoli
    valleys of chocolate mousse.

At bedtime,
I braid the sky
with my stories.

I blend
    stories of land
    stories of oceans
    stories of Pakistan.

When Ms. Grayson returns,
my stories evaporate back into the sky,
but it's okay because I get paid money.

Hardware Store—$14.99

In the aisle
next to food for cats
and food for dogs
I see the food that will make
Dadi happy—
food for birds.

In the area
at the back
that peeks outside
I use my babysitting money
to buy a pot of flowers
that will make
Dadi happy—
petunias.

Garden

On the grass that is
green
like the Pakistan flag
Dadi's mind becomes
like a pointed pencil,
sharp,
as she scoops out
the birdseed
I bought for her.

Dadi's hands
do not tremble.
Dadi's hands
are full of
purpose.
Dadi holds in
a deep breath
full of hope
and longing
before letting out a laugh
that floats.

The cardinal comes
right before sunset,
a fluttering flash
of red wings.

Deadheading

Dadi's voice is clear
as she pinches off
pouty pink petunias,
wilted blooms.
You need to get rid of
all the old
and dead flowers
to make space
for new ones.

Maybe I need to get rid
of all my old
and bad choices
to make space
for new ones?

Chess

My brother spends
too much time in his room
so I set up the chessboard
and challenge Owais.

Usually Owais wins,
but today looking at the pieces
his mouth goes into a yawn.

When I play Owais,
his mind is not on the perfect squares in front of us
but on the other shapes in his mind.

In chess,
my horse hops
my bishop bops
my queen glides everywhere.

Checkmate!

And even though I'm finally beating Owais in
    something,
it doesn't really feel good.

Junaid

At the masjid
he is the one who makes the others invisible.

Everyone seems to light up
around Junaid,
even Owais.

In the parking lot
under the basketball hoop
Junaid dribbles neatly
jumps high
swishes the ball through the net.

Nothing about Junaid
is awkward.
He moves like water.

My eyes must be drinking
because when he pauses to look at me
looking at him

I feel important
and floaty
like the ocean.

Conspirator

After Zaidu Chacha flies home,
Dadi whispers to me,
not Owais, because
he is
always in his room
lately,
because he is safer
on land
than in water,
Do you want
to go to Baskin-Robbins?
I say *Yes!*

But today,
my mouth apologizes *No* because I am struggling
to balance equations
in chemistry.
Carbon
Hydrogen
Oxygen.
I balance my voice
because that is something
I know how to do
and focus
on my work again.

But when the house
gets quiet
too quiet
because I don't hear
her Quran playing
in the back
or hear her *tasbih* beads
clicking praying clicking praying clicking praying
I get up to get
a glass of water
then run to the wide-open
front door.

Where is she?
Panic.

I run down the
cul-de-sac.
She is not there.
Up the steep hill—
she is not there.
On the walking path
I spot her curlers
her nightgown
swirling with the wind
right
and left.

I call her name
and she looks up at me.
Confused at first,
she smiles.
My heart whispers
Alhamdulillah.
Praise be to God.

The Walk Home

When we walk home
the next-door neighbor
Ms. Grayson waves hello.
Hi y'all!
She smiles with her coral-painted lips,
but not with her eyes.
And even though Dadi's mind
is unraveling,
she sees this
and returns the same
lukewarm smile.

When Ms. Grayson
pulls me to the side
and asks,
Does she speak English?
I am so angry
I want to spit.
Do you know that she reads
Yeats,
Shakespeare,
Austen?
Do you know that she has

shelves full
of books?
Do you know that she graduated
top of her class?
Do you know that she taught
English at school?
Instead, I nod,
keep walking,
and never babysit her kids
again.

Weighing Down
of Words

It happens again.
This time Dadi doesn't ask
if I want to go
to Baskin-Robbins.
This time I am reading
words heavy on my mind
and when I look up
and around
she is gone
and the front door
is open
      again.
I run down the path.

Relief.
My heart
begins to beat slower
when I see her there.

But oh no oh no oh no
her hands are holding out
rupee notes

and someone is giggling.
Aidan is behind the counter
and his smile
is not a good smile,
but a straight line
mocking her.
How can a smile
make me feel
so bad?

Aidan

When he sees me
he doesn't acknowledge me
with the crooked smile
the way he does
in science class
instead
his eyebrows rise
and his straight line
goes away
but it is too late
my fists roll up
the rupee notes
and when I guide Dadi
out the door
quick quick quick
leaving her strawberry ice cream
behind
I hear their laughter
erupt.

Decision

Ek minute
I tell Dadi
steadying her
by the door.
I remember when my tongue
betrayed Owais
I remember when my tongue
betrayed me.
I remember I need to
say something.
I go back in
to their laughter.
I find my voice
and
spit it out
It's not funny.
The store gets
Very Quiet
and I feel
light again.
I grab Dadi's ice cream.
I remember what hope
tastes like,

a little sweet
and tart
like strawberries.

The Mirror

In the mirror,
I hide my hair
    in a sparkly pink
    chiffon.
    In a dusty-orange
    cotton.
And my favorite
    an aquamarine-blue
    silk.

I study who I am
who I am becoming
who I want to be.

Before
I would have thought
what Aidan thought
what Junaid thought
what Stahr thought
what Alyson thought
but now
I care
what I think.

I care
what I say
and it feels good.

I think of Ms. White.
I grab my pencil
and
start to draw
something unexpected.
The new me.

No Longer

I no longer
speak to Aidan
in class
and the only thing
he says to me
is
Uh sorry
your grandmother
looked scary,
dry laugh.

But it is not funny
to me,
I cannot dry laugh
with him.

I wish I could
pound pound pound
the gentle cowlick
of his head
but instead I fix my eyes
on the teacher
on the board.

Instead I let Brittany
do the talking,
be his lab partner,
which she happily does
and doesn't notice me,
not once.

Lab

My anger doesn't feel
so angry,
it feels sad,
it feels lonely,
because I'm supposed
to have a partner
and I don't have one
anymore.

Trying Again

Two tables down sits
Brittany's old partner,
who looks as lost
as I feel.
Want to work with me?
A sudden smile.

Brittany's old partner
Emika
was very quiet
with Brittany
but with me
she talks talks talks
and my ears welcome
her voice.

When she turns,
her thin braid
winks at me.

Melty Circles of Joy

Stahr's eyes are leaky
with tears
while she and her mom stay at
Comfort Suites
for a few days
before moving
to their new apartment
which is no longer 8 houses away
from me
but 2 windy golf cart paths
or 3 roads away
and 6 traffic lights.

Stahr's tears stop leaking
when I lead her to the lobby,
introduce her to
Miss Polly and Miss Josefina
and to the freshly baked
chocolate chip cookies,
to melty circles
of joy.

Unwanted

After school
Stahr drives her golf cart
over to my house
and rings the bell.
She brings Mason too.

Mason, who she chooses
for a partner
in math class,
has chosen
for a partner
in real life.

Ammi gives me a look
her eyes saying
What is that boy doing here?
as she opens the door.
My face feels hot.
Too hot.

Don't you know
girls and boys can't be
just friends?

I know Ammi is thinking that.
But he is not my friend.
He is Stahr's friend.
He is Stahr's boyfriend.

Want to go with us
to Target? she asks.
No thanks,
pretty busy around here.
Got to go.
I feel relief as I shut the door
in their faces.
Ammi's gaze on me
cools.

Practice

Ammi's gaze on me warms
when I practice wearing
my hijab
a little bit
now and then
to Walmart
to Pizza Hut
other places too.
In the beginning
the looks of others spear me
but the more I wear it
the easier it becomes.
The more I wear it
the looks seem to
soften.

Spring Conferences

A kernel of an
idea
of hope
curls in my mind.

I think I would like
to try to wear it
tonight.

This time, I say:
This is my mom.
This is my dad.

This time,
I introduce them
to people.

This time,
you can see from my hijab
loosely looped
and my mother's hijab
tightly wrapped

that we are related.
Family.
The way it's meant
to be.

PART NINE

Flowering

Owais's Room

His shelf is bare
swimming medals
stuffed in a drawer
no longer smirking
at me.

Hollowness pools
inside of me.

Now what?

Without Owais

Loneliness is the color
of the swimming pool
today.

Without Owais,
I match the mood
of the pool:
Blue.

Offerings

I offer my brother
invitations to the pool
in blue and green pastels,
the colors of hope.

Come back to the
the blue cocoon.
I tell him
it's safe again.

You are my
Underwater Sibling.
Come back, please?

I bring him
a note
from Coach Kelly
urging him
to come back
to practice.

Instead he shrugs
it all away.
I like tennis, he says.

Returning

My grandfather Nana Abu does not smile
for photos,
doesn't smile on Skype either,
but
when I tell him
we are bringing Dadi back,
returning
on June 12th
for a visit,
his smile fills the screen,
his voice becomes
floating bubbles
of laughter.

My Father

It is not fair
of me to say that
my father is here
just for job security
and schools.
He is here
and we are here
because he believes
this is where
we should be.

Thirsty

But still,
I am thirsty
for home.
I want to see Nana and Nana Abu
and Asna
and everyone else.

Friends

Every Sunday,
my father wakes
at the white thread of dawn
and goes to the mosque
with food in hand
for the Breakfast Club.

Sometimes it is
warm flaky parathas,
doughy circles full of air,
scooped balls
of watermelon,
eggs that are so so spicy,
enough for six men.

And my father,
I realize,
is making friends too.

Hobbies of My Brother

Every day
after school,
Owais doesn't go with me
to the Rec Center.
Instead, he plays tennis
with his friend
Michael Lee
who lobs the ball
high
high
high
and Owais,
who always has
an eye on the ball,
smashes it
low
low
low.

And this time
if the ball goes
into the net,

he picks it right up,
dusts off the fluff,
soft and yellow,
and keeps on playing.

Who Do We Have?

I have Stahr
my mother has Penelope
Owais has Michael Lee
my father has the Breakfast Club.

Stamina

Is what you have
when you swim
back and forth
forth and back
easily without stopping.

Stamina is what I need
so I can swim
back and forth
forth and back
easily
without gasping
for air.

When Coach Kelly calls
Coffee break!
she looks right at me.
She sees me.
She throws her arms
w   i   d   e
in the air.

You can only eat an elephant
(or a whale!)
one bite at a time . . . ,
she reassures me.
You can only win a race
one breath at a time.

I can do this.
One breath at a time.

Sunday School

Here,
at the masjid,
I wear Nana's kurtas again
with piping,
3 buttons,
pockets even.

And instead of jeans,
tight denim that chokes my legs,
I wear my shalwars
soft and forgiving.

I remember the words of Nana,
When you wear hijab,
each step you take
it is as if God is smiling
upon you.

Today when I wear my hijab,
tightly wrapped,
shimmery light blue,
I can't see my hair,
and even though my face

usually envies my hair,
today when I look
in the mirror,
I think—
Not bad.

Masjid Lobby

Where boys and girls
stand
and there is no
wall partition
like there is
when we pray,
I see Owais
and Junaid.

Although they are
arguing,
it is playful
and their features
are enhanced
instead of
distorted.

I stand by Owais,
waiting.
Have I ever been
this close to Junaid
before?

If he was like Aidan,
he would put out
his hand.

I am aware of
how I stand
how I blink
how I breathe.
The shape
my mouth makes.

He has a letter-C scar
on his chin.
How did he get it?

Nurah, I know he can play basketball,
but is he as good at swimming
as he says he is?

Junaid's question
sprinkles the air.

WE both are, I say.
His eyes crinkle
into smiling
crescents.

You both are something else!
Owais smirks.

When Owais turns
to get water,
Junaid offers me
a smile,
just me,
while I tuck a smile
into my cheek.
Even though he can't see
my hair
I feel prettier than I have
in a long time
and exactly where
I'm supposed to
be.

Final Art Project

Looking through
my portfolio,
Ms. White scans through
my latest
self-portrait,
my brown
look-at-me skin
shaded with pride—
my something unexpected
me in my aquamarine
silk hijab.

Ms. White's lips dance
into a quirky smile.
Nurah, welcome to
my memory.

Final Swim Meet

Before the final swim meet,
I know what I need to do.
I walk into my brother's room.
My Underwater Sibling.

Grab his trunks,
and YELL
with my voice,
the one that made teachers
move me f   a   r   away
from Asna in class,
Enough is enough!

Fine he grumbles,
Fine he mutters,
Fine he smiles.

Coach Kelly's Warm-Up

Tan muscular arms
tracing triangles
through the air.
Freestyle.
Tan muscular arms
swirling circles
through the air.
Breaststroke.
We copy her,
stretch our doubts away.
I am ready ready ready.

Diving Block

Inside my tummy
it feels like
frogs are
hop
hop
hopping.

50 Yards

I have practiced
and practiced
over and over
back and forth
this whole season
and now have the right
rhythm for freestyle
and breast stroke.

With breast stroke,
I know to keep my arms straight together,
do a frog kick,
then circle my arms.

With free style,
I know to breathe after I've passed the flags,
glide through the water,
streamline off the wall
to speed
efficiently through
my blue cocoon.
I pat my goggles
over my eyes,

wave to Ammi
and Baba,
nod to Owais,
squeeze Stahr's arm,
and when the race begins
I am already in the water
in a perfect

d
   i
      v
        e.

Final Swim Meet

Coach Kelly's hair
is straighter than mine today
and even though I am dripping
she scoops me up
into a hug.
You did it, Nurah!
I'm so proud!
My hug makes
the tips of her hair
curl up into smiles.

And Ammi
and Baba
are looking at me,
faces light and loose and lovey
because I am in third place,
a winner
of a medal.

Owais's Turn

The pool welcomes him,
acts like he's never been gone,
and he swims
so beautifully
so swiftly.
Even though I'm
out of breath
from doing laps,
watching him
still takes my breath
away.

Medal

It is the perfect
amount of heavy
and hangs on the hook
on my wall
and on my heart
in my body.

Newspaper

In the city gazette
is a picture
of the team
me on the lower right
next to Stahr
holding my medal.

I
snip
snip
snip
the paper rectangle
out
carefully
to show Nana and Nana Abu
and Asna and
family back home.

I highlight my name
in yellow,
show it to Dadi.
When she asks me
my name,
I point to it
proudly.

Summer

Suitcases being zipped up,
full and fat,
when the bell rings.

Visitor

The man who is missing one arm
Mr. Tim
holds out the smell of cinnamon.
My wife b-b-b-baked cookies.

Thank you, says Owais.
My father e x t e n d s his hand.
Please come in.

But Mr. Tim shakes his head
and smiles,
how different he looks
with a smile on his face.
*Sure fine d-d-d-daughter
you got there . . .*
He waves,
and this is the first time
I notice
a wedding ring on the fourth finger
of his right hand.
Glinting in the sunlight.

Teatime

My mother delicately
nibbles Mr. Tim's cookie,
then smiles and rests
her hands,
with the tips of her nails
bitten into
crescent moons,
onto her belly,
which is full and fat.

This time,
the baby is the size
of a mango,
my favorite fruit.

For My Mother

My father presents
a bouquet
of white flowers
so tiny
and faint
like tissue paper.
Baby's breath, she says,
her eyes smiling
so hard
her mouth
is jealous.

So

Do you like it here?
asks Baba
and Owais
answers an
I guess so
but not before
he tucks
a smile
inside his cheek,
making all of us
smile
smile
smile.

Windy Day

My father
sometimes reads people
well,
but he reads the wind
very well.

On windy days,
when the trees dance,
my father calls us
and we watch
his kite
unfurl on a long
long
long
piece of thread
until it kisses the sky.

And even though
the trees here are taller,
the houses too,
my father makes the kite
dance easily in the wind.

Trim little circles,
zigzags
too.

In those moments,
when I dive into
my blue cocoon,
soar through the water,
I become the kite—
free.

Author's Note

Although this story is fictional, I drew on my experiences from when I moved from Abu Dhabi, the United Arab Emirates, to Peachtree City, Georgia. Like Nurah, I joined a team—not swimming, but a tennis team, and found those experiences shaped and challenged me. I barely made the team, but got much better with consistent practice. Full disclosure—like Owais, my three brothers excelled at the sport much more than I did!

Like Nurah's, my grandmother, who was highly educated, struggled with Alzheimer's and did not remember my name anymore. I still remember the numb sadness I felt watching her decline, and tried to show it through Nurah's eyes.

Like Nurah's father, my father followed the school bus to our school on our first day of high school to make sure we reached it safely. I rode a bus where the bus monitor was missing an arm and was picked on by some students. I remember the horror I felt. I remember wishing I could say something to help. Alas, I did not my find my voice, but my eldest brother did. The day the students teased the monitor asking if he wore a wedding ring was the day my eldest brother broke his silence and yelled at the other students to SHUT UP. I remember feeling elation mixed with fear. I worried that we would become easy targets the next day, but amazingly the students stopped picking on the bus monitor. To this day, I think saying something, *anything*, to help someone who is being picked on mercilessly is better than just sitting there and being a silent witness.

I was a senior in high school the year the September 11 tragedy occurred. Unbeknownst to us, an officer from Homeland Security stopped by to interrogate my father. Luckily, my father was eventually left alone, but that is not the case for others. Unfortunately, there are criminals who commit terrorist attacks citing Islam, a religion of peace, as a reason. For Muslim students, it can be mortifying to go to school the day after a terrorist attack has been committed by someone touting Islam. The day after September 11, I was not picked on, but one of my best friends, who was born and raised in the United States, who also wore a hijab, was picked on and told to go back to her country. Owais's line in my story "I'm not a fighter" was inspired by my cousin who said this courageous line when he was picked on by high school bullies in the locker room.

I started to wear my hijab in high school on a

Wednesday in tenth grade, but like Nurah I practiced wearing it first to regular places like Pizza Hut and Walmart. I think wearing anything that makes you look different, especially when all you want to do is blend in, can be quite challenging. I admire those who choose to be different in a country where it is not common and appreciate all those who support these students, whether it's simply being a friend or treating them exactly the way you would want to be treated.

I also remember sitting alone at lunch and how different my school experience was when a girl asked if I would like to eat lunch with her. Having a friend believe in you, like Stahr and Nurah do for each other, is life changing. Thank you to all those who invite others to eat lunch with them—it makes a world of a difference.

Glossary

alhamdulillah: Praise be to God

aloo kabab: potato and ground beef mixed together and then dipped in egg yolk, coated in bread crumbs, and then fried to make a crispy patty

assalamualaikum: Muslim greeting for "peace be upon you"

biryani: spicy meat and rice cooked separately before being layered and cooked together

Chacha: Urdu word for paternal uncle, specifically father's younger brother

dadi: paternal grandmother

dal: lentils

dupatta: a shawl-like scarf women in Pakistan wear over their shalwar kameez and worn over the kurta. It can be draped over the head or chest.

ek: Urdu word for *one*

ghee: clarified butter made from the milk of a buffalo or cow, used in South Asian cooking

halal: "permissible" in Arabic. For food, it typically means meat that is specially butchered with Islamic guidelines. For fish, the guidelines are more lenient, which is why Nurah gets fish fillets from McDonald's.

hijab: headscarf Muslim women or girls may wear

istikhara: prayer recited by Muslims when in need of guidance on an issue in their life

jaldi se: Urdu words for *quickly*

kajal: powdery eyeliner that women wear in Pakistan

khichri: rice and lentils cooked together until soft. It is cooked extra soft for babies.

kurta: loose, flowy Pakistani top. Girls' clothes are usually colorful.

masjid: Muslim place of worship

mehndi: henna paste that temporarily dyes hands, usually drawn on hands to celebrate events, but can also be put on for big moments, such as Nurah moving, in this case!

motia: tiny white flowers that appear at the start of summer and bloom joyously in shades of white. These flowers are often threaded together to form bracelets or necklaces in Karachi, Pakistan, and South Asia.

namaz: Urdu word for the obligatory Muslim prayers that occur five times a day. In Arabic, the word for prayer is Salah.

nana: maternal grandfather (Nurah calls her maternal grandmother Nana, though, since it was Owais's first word)

nani: maternal grandmother

paratha: delicious flatbread consisting of layers of cooked dough

rupee: Pakistani unit of money

samosa: a fried or baked pastry with a savory filling, such as spiced potatoes, onions, peas, meat, or lentils

sari: an outfit worn by South Asian women that is made of several yards of lightweight cloth. It's draped so that one end makes a skirt and the other is typically a shoulder covering.

shalwars: loose, flowy Pakistani pants

Surah Al-Kahf: the 18th chapter of the Quran. Al-Kahf means "The Cave."

tasbih: prayer beads

wa-alaikum-as-salaam: Muslim reply to *assalamualaikum*, meaning "peace be upon you too"

Nurah's Aloo Kabab
Lunch Recipe

Ingredients:

6 medium potatoes
1 pound ground beef
1 teaspoon salt
1 teaspoon ground cumin
1 teaspoon ginger paste
1 teaspoon garlic paste
½ teaspoon ground coriander
½ teaspoon ground red pepper
2 eggs, beaten
1 cup bread crumbs
Vegetable oil

1. Peel and boil the potatoes (aloo) until soft for approximately 25 minutes and mash separately.
2. Cook the ground beef until brown. To the beef add the salt, ground cumin, ginger, garlic, ground coriander, and red pepper.
3. Mix the mashed potatoes and browned ground beef evenly.
4. Shape the mixture into circular kabab shapes with your hands.

5. Dip kababs into the beaten egg.
6. Coat kababs with bread crumbs.
7. Shallow fry in medium-heat oil. Flip the kababs over to ensure they are golden brown on each side.* Enjoy! They are delicious served with rice or naan bread.

*Tip: Freeze the kababs first if you can for a couple of hours, as it makes frying easier and the kababs will be less likely to break apart.

Storage:
If you have any extra kababs, they can be stored in the freezer. They can be cooked quickly or jaldi se by shallow frying them in vegetable oil.

Acknowledgments

A huge thank-you to:

Agent Rena Rossner: for offering representation when I was queried out, for your vision in taking my Microsoft Word document and seeing it as a book, for pushing me to dig deeper, for offering insightful edits, for your speedy submission, and for being up at all hours during the auction. I'm so grateful for you! Thank you for your energy and passion and above all, for *believing* in Nurah and me. I can't thank you enough.

Editor Alyson Day: for falling in love with my story, for yelling on the subway when I accepted the offer, and for championing Nurah in the best way. I couldn't have asked for a more enthusiastic editor. Thank you for your uplifting comments throughout my story. I live for your supportive emails, your gorgeous insights, and can't wait for more book journeys with you!

The *entire* Harper team: Soumbal Qureshi and Molly Fehr for giving me a dreamy cover and beautiful interior art! Shona McCarthy and the copyediting team for meticulous edits, Eva Lynch-Comer for my countless emails, Meghan Petit and Allison Brown for gorgeous production, Emma Meyer and Lauren Levite for enthusiastic marketing and publicity.

Editors Audrey Maynard and Ann Rider for support and making me feel like my stories mattered from the beginning.

All My SCBWI Critique Partners who responded when I was just a stranger emailing and who gave me constant hope throughout the *long* writing process, especially Melissa Miles, Amy Board, Vicki Wilson, Tresha Render, Becky Goodman, and my first family readers: Sana Dossul for always being so kind and ready to read, Huma Faruqi, and Asna Dossul.

My Author Friends and Blurbers: Veera Hiranandani, Aisha Saeed, Hena Khan, Rajani LaRocca, Aya Khalil, Saadia Faruqi, Saira Mir, Marzieh Abbas, and Becky Sayler for being there at all hours!

Ilse Craane and Kendra Marcus, my previous agents, for telling me numerous times to write middle grade (I listened!) and for encouraging me while this book was in its broken stages.

My eleventh grade English teacher—Mrs. Patricia Carman for transforming me by giving me the gift of writing and for your inspiring "coffee breaks."

These supportive groups: Rena's Renegades, #DiverseDreamers, #MGBookChat, #the21ders

Author Jasmine Warga, whose novel in verse gave me the boost I needed to finish mine.

Eliot VanValkenburg, Aisha Zakaria, and Dr. Amena

Dossul for swimming expertise.

My BFFs, Salma Stoman, Sarah Stoman, and Saira Pasha for coaxing me out of my writing cocoon for dinner six feet apart outside, laughter, and endless memories.

My courageous cousin Noor Faruqi for sharing your locker room incident with me.

My Whole Family (including all my twenty-five cousins!) in Peachtree City, in Pakistan, and beyond.

Mom and Abajan (Mrs. Nazia Malik and Dr. Firasat Malik), Daado-Jan (Mrs. Ismat Malik): Love and Duas. Abajan, thanks for comparing tea to the color of your skin; it inspired me!

Cousins Dr. Amena Dossul and Asna Dossul for being my sisters, my BFFS, my everything, and whose names I will trace on the beach sand for the rest of my life.

My three brothers, Hamzah, Talha, and Osman: I don't know who I would be without you.

—Hamzah, for standing up for the man on the bus and for always being so kind.

—Talha, for saying you always thought I'd be a writer: it spurred me on more than you thought. Thank you for always cooking for us (even though my butter chicken tastes better.)

—Osman, thanks for complimenting my writing once. Means a lot coming from you! ☺

Nana (Mrs. Zarina Zakaria), so much of this book I thought of you. Thank you for always gifting us the perfect clothes. I love your love for nature. Since Nana Abu's death, I am in awe of your strength.

My parents, Amma and Abba (Mrs. Huma and Mr. Zaheer Faruqi), for coming over, watching the children, emptying the dish rack, providing me aloo kababs, and for shaping me into who I am. Amma, special thanks for Wednesdays. Abba, thanks for your stories and love for kites. You both made moving continents look easy. Without you, I would have a very messy home and still be working on this book.

My husband, Naoman Malik, for reading my story early on, saying I had stars and just needed to make them into a constellation, and for printing out my *many* manuscripts over the years! Thank you x infinity for making sacrifices, BIG and small, so I could write.

My daughters Zineera, Anisa, Hanifa for cleaning, baking, joyous chaos, and for being the reason why I have to get off my computer. I pray you wear your faith proudly.

My first American friend, Chelsea Hartt-Baudhuin, who said those eight words, "Do you want to eat lunch with me?" It changed everything.